...ble
and Maggie

GIVE AND TAKE

Jessie Haas
illustrated by Alison Friend

CANDLEWICK PRESS

To Karen Pryor,
who's taught us all so much
about give and take

J. H.

For Charlotte and Pearl

A. F.

Text copyright © 2013 by Jessie Haas
Illustrations copyright © 2013 by Alison Friend

First edition 2013

Library of Congress Catalog Card Number 2012942618
ISBN 978-0-7636-5021-6

13 14 15 16 17 18 SCP 10 9 8 7 6 5 4 3 2 1

Printed in Humen, Dongguan, China

This book was typeset in Dante.
The illustrations were done in gouache.

Candlewick Press
99 Dover Street
Somerville, Massachusetts 02144

visit us at www.candlewick.com

CHAPTER ONE

Give and Take

Maggie said, "Let's go for a ride, Bramble!"

Bramble knew about rides. The rider sat in the saddle. The horse did all the hard work.

Maggie brushed Bramble and braided her mane.

She cleaned Bramble's hooves and squirted her with bug spray.

She put the saddle on Bramble's back.

She pulled the girth under Bramble's belly.

Bramble took a deep breath. The air filled up her belly, big and fat.

She held the breath in.

"This girth fit you before!" Maggie said.

Then she looked at Bramble's face.

"Bramble," Maggie said, "are you bloating?"

Bramble kept holding her breath.
It wasn't easy. She stared straight ahead,
hardly blinking. Her nose wrinkled.
Her lips twitched.

"I know what to do about that," Maggie
said. She led Bramble in a circle. Bramble
held her breath for a few steps. Then she
had to let it out — *whoosh!*

"Thank you, Bramble," Maggie said.
"You look so slim!"

Maggie tried to
put the bridle over
Bramble's nose.
Bramble held
her head high.

Maggie stood
on a hay bale.
Bramble held
her head even
higher.

"Bramble!" Maggie said. "Don't you want to meet the neighbors? Don't you want to explore?"

Explore? That sounded good.

But Bramble didn't think she should always do what Maggie wanted. Neither of them should be boss all the time. There should be some give-and-take.

She kept her head high. She kept her mouth shut.

Maggie pulled out her horse book and read. She got an idea.

"Okay," she said. "If you put your head down, Bramble, I'll give you a carrot."

Bramble sniffed the air. Did Maggie really have a carrot?

Yes.

Bramble lowered her head. Maggie gave her a carrot, and Bramble took it. She let Maggie put on the bridle.

This was better. Give and take.

They started down the street. Bramble
had a bounce in her step. Her hooves went
clip-clop-clip, all around the block.

"This is my new horse, Bramble," Maggie
told everyone she met. She loved saying
the words.

One neighbor was working in his garden. "This is my new horse, Bramble," Maggie told him. "Bramble, this is Mr. Dingle. You can see his garden and his henhouse over your fence."

Mr. Dingle patted Bramble. "What a nice, quiet horse," he said. "I'm sure she'll be a good neighbor."

CHAPTER TWO

Too Quiet

On Monday morning, an alarm clock buzzed in the house. Maggie raced out. She dumped grain in Bramble's bucket. She filled the water pail. She cleaned the stall.

Then Maggie rushed inside.

"Eat quick, Maggie! It's time for the bus!"

"I'm hurrying, I'm hurrying!"

Feet thundered. Things crashed.

Maggie's mother dashed to the car.

"Good-bye, Bramble."

Maggie ran to meet the bus.

"See you this afternoon, Bramble!"

Maggie's father hopped onto his

motorbike. "See you later, Bramble."

Suddenly it was quiet. Too quiet.

A bug bit Bramble. There was no Maggie to spray on bug spray.

Bramble swished her tail. She scratched her neck on a tree. She stuck her nose in her feed bucket.

Finally she put her head over the fence
and watched Mr. Dingle.

She tasted a rose.

"Stop!" said Mr. Dingle. He nailed
a rail on top of the fence.

Bramble reached through the fence. She
sampled a daylily.

"*Please stop!*"

Bramble chewed the fence.

"Please, please, *please* stop!"

Mr. Dingle sprayed something bad-tasting

on the fence rails.

Then he stretched out in his chair.

He closed his eyes. After a while,

he snored.

Bramble looked down the driveway.

No Maggie. No anybody.

Bramble yawned.

Just then a hen flew into Mr. Dingle's garden. She scratched with her strong yellow feet. She tossed dirt and plants in the air. She made a hole and took a dust bath in it.

Mr. Dingle woke up and saw the hen. He chased her. They squashed more plants.

Finally, Mr. Dingle caught the hen and put her back in the coop.

It was the only interesting thing that happened all day.

Finally the car drove in. Maggie's mother
got out. "Hi, Bramble."

The bus stopped at the corner. Maggie
ran up the driveway. Bramble whinnied

22

"I'm glad to see you too," Maggie said. "I saved you my apple core. I drew this picture in art class. This is me, and this is you."

Bramble ate the apple core. She looked at the picture.

Then she looked at her saddle and bridle.

"You're right, Bramble," Maggie said. "Let's go!"

CHAPTER THREE

Sshhoosshhh!

Maggie got Bramble ready. Bramble carried Maggie down the street, around a corner, down another street. Her hooves went *clip-clop-clip*.

But there was another sound. *Sshhooshh! Sshooshh!*

They came to an open gate. The strange sound was louder here.

SSHHOSSHHH!

SSHHOOSSHHH!

After a few steps, Bramble stopped. What *was* that sound? Was it an animal? It must be huge!

"Do you need another carrot, Bramble?" Maggie asked. "Take a step first."

Bramble took a step. Maggie gave her a carrot. Step, carrot. Step, carrot. Slowly they went toward the sound.

When they came out into the open,

Bramble stopped again.

She had never seen a place like this. So

much sky and sand. So much *water*!

The water moved. It made a noise.

Bramble was used to water that stayed still.

She was used to water in a bucket.

"Don't be afraid, Bramble," Maggie said.

She got off. "See? I'll show you."

Maggie walked forward. Bramble followed. The water came toward them. It curled up and up—

SSHHOOSSHHH! It curled over and crashed onto the sand.

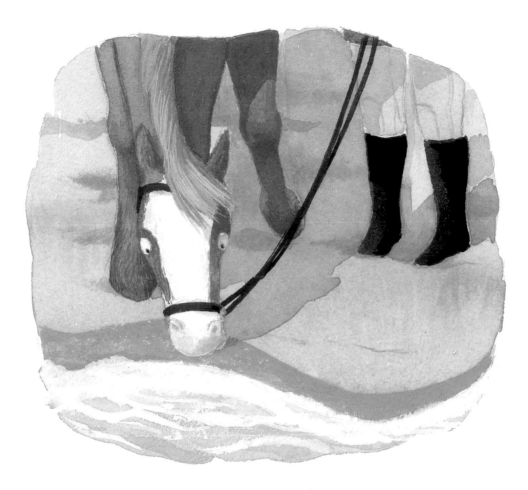

Then — *swwisshhh!* — it slid back,
bubbling and foaming.

Bramble followed it.

"Careful, Bramble," Maggie said.
"You'll get—"

SSHHOOSSHHH! In came another wave.

"Splashed," Maggie said.

Swwisshhh. The water slid away.

Another wave came in—

SSHHOOSSHHH! It foamed around

Bramble's legs. She put her head down.

She tasted it.

Salty. Not good to drink.

But it was good to watch. It was good

to smell.

It was wonderful to splash in.

"Aaaggh!" Maggie said. "I'm all wet!"

Waves came and went.

Came and went.

Give, take.

SSHHOOSSHHH! Swwisshhh.

CHAPTER FOUR
The Hen

On Tuesday, Bramble was alone again.

She was so bored, she whinnied at cars on

the street. Every car. All day. She whinnied

at Mr. Dingle. She whinnied at the hen.

On Tuesday evening, Mr. Dingle came to
Maggie's house. He brought a dozen eggs.
"Your horse seems unhappy," he said.
"She makes a lot of noise."

Maggie said, "Horses are herd animals.
They like company. Maybe I should stay
home from school and keep Bramble
company."

"No," said Mom.

"We could get a goat," Maggie said.
"Horses like goats."

Mr. Dingle frowned. "Goats climb fences,"
he said. "They eat gardens."

Then he looked excited. "How about a hen? I have a hen I could give you."

"Thank you," Maggie's mother said. "But we can't take your hen."

"This hen gets out a lot," Mr. Dingle said.

"Maybe she will wander over to your yard.

I hope she doesn't. But she might."

On Tuesday night, Bramble had a visitor.

When Maggie came out Wednesday morning, she said, "Mom! Dad! Mr. Dingle's hen has wandered over here."

"I was afraid she would!" Mom said.

Bramble ate her grain. The hen ate the crumbs that Bramble dropped.

Bramble did not approve. She always cleaned up her own crumbs.

Bramble went out to eat grass. The hen followed. She ate some of Bramble's grass.

Bramble didn't approve of that, either. She followed and watched, followed and watched, until she couldn't stand it anymore.

Bramble sneaked up. She blew her breath under the hen's feathers.

BRAWKK!!

The hen flew up in Bramble's face.

Bramble jumped back in surprise.

The hen settled her feathers. *Peck!* She ate another blade of Bramble's grass.

Bramble couldn't believe it! She sneaked up again, ready to blow at the hen.

Then Bramble saw something amazing.

The hen ate a bug!

Bramble watched closely. The hen ate all the time. Grass. Bug. Bug. Grass. Bug, bug, bug. Grass. She made friendly noises. *Oohh-cluck-cluck-cluck. Ohh-cluck.*

All day, Bramble followed the hen.

They ate together.

They both took dust baths. They had naps. So did Mr. Dingle.

Maggie came home. Mr. Dingle was leaning on the fence.

"I'll help you catch your hen," Maggie said.

"No, no!" said Mr. Dingle. "I'm giving her to Bramble."

"But I don't know how to take care of a hen," Maggie said.

"It's easy," Mr. Dingle said. "Here's some grain for her." He handed Maggie a bag.

"A hen also needs a perch," he said.

"She's got one!" Maggie said.

"And a hen needs a nest."

Maggie said, "She's got one of those, too!"

"A hen also needs somewhere to scratch that isn't my garden! Please," Mr. Dingle said.

"Take her. We will all be much happier."

"Okay. And thank you."

Maggie scattered some grain on the ground. The hen flapped down to eat it. Bramble pushed the hen to one side. She ate some grain, too. That was fair. Give and take.